SNOOPY'S
ABC's

Peanuts® characters created
and drawn by Charles M. Schulz

Text by Nancy Hall

Background illustrations by Art and Kim Ellis

A GOLDEN BOOK • NEW YORK

Western Publishing Company, Inc., Racine, Wisconsin 53404

Aa

A is for **angry**

and **artist**

and **armor.**

Bb

B is for **beagle**

and **Belle**—a real charmer!

Cc

C is for **cake**

and **carry**

and **cry.**

Dd

D is for **dirty**

and **desert** that's **dry**.

Ee

E is for **earphones**

and **Easter egg,**
too.

Ff

F is for **footprint**
made by you-know-who.

Gg

G is for **golf club**

and **globe**
of the world.

Hh

H, as you see, is for
hair that is curled.

Ii

I is for **ice cream**—

chocolate, I hope.

Jj

J is for **jack-o'-lantern,**

jump rope,

and **joke.**

Kk

SMAK!

K is for **kiss**

and **kite** with a tail.

Ll

L is for **laughing**

US MAIL

and **letters** you mail.

Mm

M is for **music**

and **marching** out west.

Nn

N is for **notes**,

newspaper,

and **nest**.

Oo

O is for **overcoat**
made out of wool.

Pp

P is for **pumpkin patch**

and **present** to **pull**.

Qq

Q is for **quarrel**

and **question**—
like "Why?"

Rr

R is for **rainbow**
that colors the sky.

Ss

S is for **snowman**

and **spots**

and a **sled**.

Tt

T is for **tennis**

and a **tractor** that's red.

Uu   U's for **umbrella**.

It keeps off the rain.

Vv

V's for **vacation**—
I may go to Spain.

TO AIRPORT

Ww

W's for **witch**

and **wet** to the bone.

Xx

X, as you know,
is for **xylophone**.

Yy

So now we are left
with **yo-yo** for **Y**.

And last comes **Z**,
so I'll say good-bye!